T0145055

Rudy Rabbit Tried

Written and Illustrated by
Elliott Gilbert

Rudy Rabbit Tried

To order additional copies of this book, contact:
Xlibris
844-714-8691
www.Xlibris.com
Orders@Xlibris.com

ISBN: Softcover   978-1-6698-0292-1
         Hardcover   978-1-6698-0293-8
         EBook   978-1-6698-0291-4

Library of Congress Control Number: 2021924910

Print information available on the last page.

Rev. date: 12/10/2021

Tried

Written and Illustrated by

Elliott Gilbert

Rudy, we can't go on like this much longer ... you must find yourself a career!

Rudy's family was desperate. His ever-increasing family required more food. Now Rudy couldn't just scrape by— he had to go out and work hard to support his children.

One day Rudy gathered his family together and explained that although his prospects were uncertain, he must try. And so Rudy went off seeking work.

As he began looking, he thought, "What can I do?" Rudy was pretty good at arithmetic, and so he first tried a bank. But he was turned down.

Rudy thought to himself again. "I'm a pretty good saleman. I could sell almost anything." So he tried just that. He was offered a position selling books.

And that was very frustrating, because when Rudy tried high pitch selling, it came out as low pitch squeaking.

Every day Rudy returned to his family with nothing to report. And although he would try to sound encouraging, all seemed hopeless.

What could Rudy try next?
Well, he was a pretty good cook. Maybe he could try a restaurant. He tried that, but that didn't work out either.

It was most discouraging. Rudy had tried, but maybe he just wasn't qualified to do anything. Or worse, could it be that he wasn't very smart? Certainly he had tried and tried, but trying, though important, was not enough. Something was missing.

The situation was most distressing to Rudy. Every day was the same. Nothing.

"I need a change" Rudy thought. So he went to a nearby playground and played his favorite game—basketball. He was very good at it, and it was fun. As it happened, a basketball coach was close-by who noticed how good Rudy really was. In fact the coach was so impressed, he offered Rudy a starting position on his professional basketball team.

Now Rudy is the star player on his team.

Everyone admires his special talent.

Who knows, maybe were it not for the coach, Rudy would still be trying.

Sometimes we can all use help.

ELLIOTT GILBERT has illustrated and written numerous other children's picture books, including *Max Goes Hunting*, *My Cat Story*, *Mittens in May* by Maxine Kumin, and *The Best Loved Doll* by Rebecca Caudill. His paintings have been exhibited in many galleries, and won numerous awards. Examples of his work can be seen on his website, elliottgilbert.com. He lives with his wife in Hoboken, New Jersey.

ALSO BY ELLIOTT GILBERT

When Max the Marten is old enough, his parents teach him how to hunt for his own food. Max is excited and proud. But when he goes out hunting for the first time, he quickly discovers that the carnivorous life may not be for him. Max Goes Hunting is a charming little tale about growing up and trying to live up to the expectations of your family--and of yourself.

ISBN: 978-1482366655 • $9.95

Available at Amazon.com

MY CAT STORY

illustrated by ELLIOTT GILBERT

A day in the life of a mama cat and her kittens, told entirely in pictures. Perfect for reading to little ones because you can change the story every time, or let them tell the story!

ISBN: 978-1481801690 • $8.95

Available at Amazon.com

Printed in the United States
by Baker & Taylor Publisher Services